pasta   Cheap, filling food made from flour,
             eggs and water. The dough is made into
             many different shapes and can be called
             names like spaghetti, ravioli, and lasagne
             It can be used in many delicious
             recipes

piazza   A square or plaza in a city

presepio   A Christmas crib or manger. A scene
             representing the story of the First
             Christmas in Bethlehem. St. Francis of
             Assisi made the first presepio for the
             people of Greccio, Italy, about 700 years
             ago

strada   Street

trattoria A restaurant. Pasta would usually be
             on the menu at a trattoria

MOON-EYES

MOON-EYES

Jean Chapman

Illustrated by Astra Lacis

McGRAW-HILL BOOK COMPANY
New York   St. Louis   San Francisco

Library of Congress Cataloging in Publication Data

Chapman, Jean.
    Moon-eyes.

    SUMMARY: A stray cat sets out through the streets
of Rome in search of the small child that showed him
some kindness.
    [1. Cats — Fiction. 2. Rome — Fiction] I. Lācis,
Astra. II. Title.
PZ7.C369Mo   [E]   79-22088
ISBN 0-07-010648-7

First distribution in the United States of America 1980 by McGraw-Hill Book
Company.
First published in 1978 by Hodder and Stoughton Pty Limited, Australia.
This edition published by arrangement with Hodder and Stoughton (Australia) Pty Limited.

Text © 1978 Jean Chapman
Illustrations © 1978 Astra Lacis

123456789   876543210

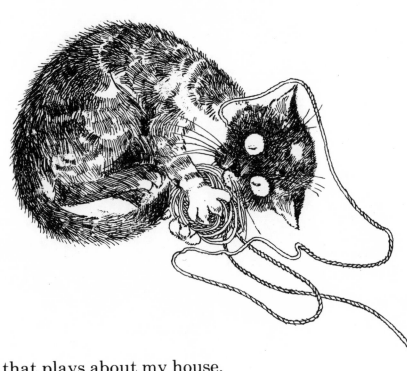

A cat,
I keep, that plays about my house,
Grown fat,
With eating many a miching mouse.

Robert Herrick

It was late, in fact close to midnight, when the Cat
Woman shuffled out of the piazza. She was carrying
a bucket of steaming pasta, which she slopped in
spoonfuls to the waiting cats. They had run to her,
padding silently out of the shadowy darkness of the
Forum, to crowd about her in fawning circles. A
tangle of heads and tails, they mewed their pussy
songs of cupboard love.

So many cats!

All of them were scraggy. There were gray cats and orange cats. Black cats and tabbies. There were fat-faced cats, low-slung mother cats and kittens, and skinny, rheumaticky old cats, along with the down-and-outs: the shabby cats with lumps of fur missing from their coarse coats. Many others wore the scars from yowling cat fights; so there were cats with ragged ears, cats with weepy eyes, and cats with limping legs . . . And every cat was hungry.

A struggle for food began as the first spoonful of the pasta left the bucket. The cats spat and hissed now, and they pushed and nudged, shouldered and strained in frantic haste to gobble up as much of the thick white blobs of pasta as possible. A great deal was snatched away, even before it had slid from the spoon. And, if it did fall on a furry back or head, that was wolfed down by an obliging neighbor before there was time to twitch a whisker.

A thin black cat scrabbled hopefully with the rest. Several times he had almost reached the Cat Woman. With each try he was bullied out of the way by the fast-moving experts. A small cat, he was easily shoved to the edge of the cat crowd. In the end, he was forced to circle around the edge, to follow the journeys of the pasta spoon with his large eyes. Eyes as round and as yellow as a pale full moon! Then, and it was wonderful luck, a spoonful of the pasta flipped over the cats' heads to dollop down beside him.

Instantly, Moon-Eyes was upon it. But before he could eat, without any warning, claws flashed down on him and viciously scratched his nose. Blood dribbled from torn fur and flesh. Moon-Eyes flinched with pain. He drew back, hardly more than a paw's length. It was far enough for his attacker, a greedy old tabby, to duck down her head, swivel it sideways and swiftly suck up his pasta. And while she ate, she growled. She threatened Moon-Eyes, warning him to keep away.

Moon-Eyes was not to be easily defeated — he counter-attacked. In he came, diving low to one side, to retrieve his meal. Old Tab pulled back now, with a string of pasta hanging from her mouth, and as she retreated, she gulped it down. Moon-Eyes was beaten.

He was still unfed when the Cat Woman went back across the piazza with her empty bucket.

Gradually the cats left too, returning to the ruins of the Forum. They disappeared into their sleeping holes, or hunted for mice amongst the broken pillars and arches, or for anything that moved in the crannies secreted in the huge slabs of stone and marble. And there were other affairs needing cat attention, so some prowled into nearby streets on nightly examination of the dust-bins, or a trip over rooftops.

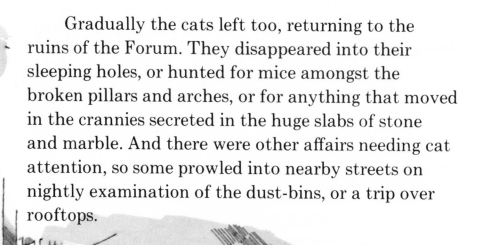

Hunger kept Moon-Eyes where he was. He mooched about the deserted street, and finally, he did nose out a forgotten dab of dried pasta. It was the remains of an earlier feeding, and it must have been days old. Cold and stale, stiff and chewy, the pasta had lain hidden on the stone curbing which supported the thin iron bars of a fence. Moon-Eyes slowly chewed through its tastelessness, his large eyes glinting restlessly. He was alert, very watchful for any signs of a cat-thief, such as sneaky old Tab.

However, he was able to eat undisturbed. When he'd finished his meal, he leisurely licked a paw to clean his face. Gingerly, he wiped the drying blood from his scratched nose, then he stepped neatly through the bars of the fence to a narrow ledge of rock. It was high above the Forum and jutted out from the coping to make a cat-sized veranda. He hunkered down there, folding his forepaws under his chest. His head was tucked against his bony shoulders and his eyelids drooped, until they closed into slits like finely crayoned lines that were darker than his fur.

Moon-Eyes was contented and comfortable, even for a Forum cat. The coping gave him protection from the bleak wind, as well as the scuds of misty rain that had begun to fall. It also hid him from the street.

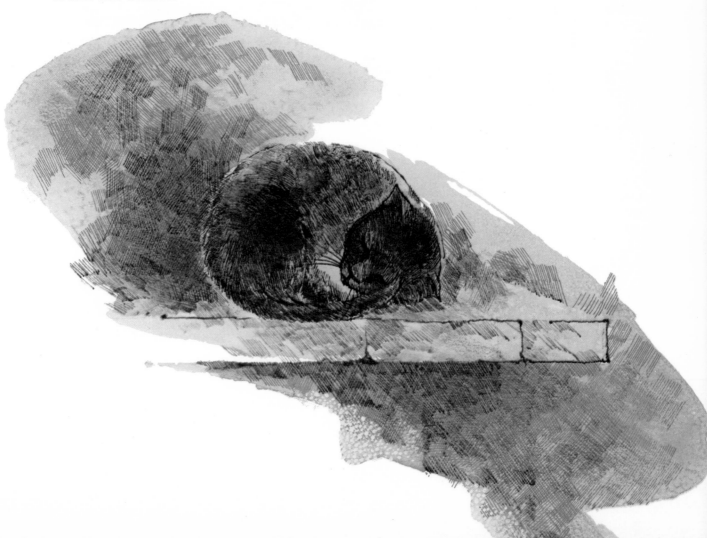

By morning, the rain had cleared, but it was still cold — almost cold enough to snow. Thin sunshine was luring the cats from their hiding-holes. About seven of them had taken possession of the sand-stoned terrace with its grassed edgings, which lay below Moon-Eyes' ledge.

The fastidious cats were washing faces and cleaning fur, smoothing each hair into perfect order. The idle ones sprawled untidily in the frail warmth of the sun, as lazy as people drowsing on a summer-hot beach.

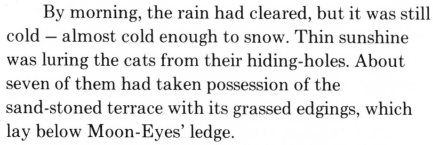

Like a prince in exile, a Siamese cat stalked up to the group, to sit a little apart from the others. His stare may have been slightly cross-eyed, but it was regal and aloof as he posed his head and held his back stiffly straight. It was this cat, and the other half-wild strays, that a woman came to sketch.

A little girl was with her, and while the woman's pencil swept back and forth over her drawing pad, she half-listened to the child's chatter.

After a while, the little girl climbed up onto the coping on Moon-Eyes' fence. She gripped the iron bars, then crabbed along towards his ledge. Moon-Eyes didn't move. If he stayed where he was, she might not notice him. She discovered him a moment later.

"There's a cat right here!" the child called out. "Awh! You've got a scratched nose," she told Moon-Eyes as she jumped from the coping to squat down on her side of the fence. "He's got a sore nose, Mumma!" she called out again.

"Mmmm!" the woman answered without looking up.

The child wriggled, edging closer to the coping until she was no more than two tails' length from the cat. Then, she used her teeth to drag off a red woolen glove. The bared hand was thrust through the iron bars to reach out towards Moon-Eyes' head. He stiffened. With her first touch he tensed with alarm, ready to bound away with hisses and spits. Instead, fear held Moon-Eyes to the ledge. There was no way to escape. He was trapped on the ledge. The child was blocking his return to the street, and the terrace was too far below him.

The only course left to the cat was to wait for a chance to bound somehow past the girl, to the street.

His ears, cardboard flat, lay against his head. His claws unsheathed. The pupils of his eyes rounded into huge circles. His neck craned, his body strained forwards and the waving tip of his tail signaled his mistrust.

They were desperate, knotted seconds for the cat. The child's stroking went on soothingly, confidently. To the rocking, backwards-and-forwards rhythm of her hand she began to croon above his head, "Poor-little-cat-little-black-cat-poor-little-cat-little-black-cat!"

She sang and she stroked; she sang and she stroked. The sing-song repetition of her words and the caresses were like a binding spell.

The little girl felt the warmth of the cat's thin body under her hand. She felt the ridged hardness of his spine under the fur and she watched with interest as his large eyes shrank to half-moons, then upwards into narrow golden slits.

Slowly, very slowly the cat's body was softening. He sank back into a more comfortable position. Moon-Eyes was giving in to the pleasure of the stroking. He was spellbound. Suddenly, a purr, hardly louder than a whisper, rattled from his throat. The sound seemed to surprise the cat more than it did the child.

"He's purring, Mumma! Look at him, Mumma!" she called out. "The little cat's purring! He's nice! Look at him, Mumma!"

"Mmmm!" answered the woman again. She looked up. Down went the sketch book. She plunged across the short space between them, gathered up the little girl and pulled her hand back through the bars. "You shouldn't have touched that cat, Maria!" she scolded. "You shouldn't have touched it! It's dirty! It's a stray! It could be sick and make you sick! Did it scratch you, Bambina?" she asked anxiously. She looked at Maria's hand, turning it about, inspecting it.

"No, of course, he didn't!" Maria assured her mother, and taking her hand away looked at it herself. "See? No scratches!"

"That's lucky! He's a Forum cat, Bambina. A wild stray. He may never have been touched by anyone before. You really are lucky not to be scratched, and we must find somewhere you can wash straight away." The woman fussed and a protesting Maria was hurried away from the fence and Moon-Eyes.

Moon-Eyes wanted the smooth feeling, the contentment that had come with the stroking, to go on, and on. This inner warmth was new to him. It was as comforting as a full belly.

Moon-Eyes propped his forepaws on the coping. He stared wide-eyed and trustingly after Maria. She went out of his view into an alley, and he jumped lightly to the coping, paused there briefly, then flipped down to the pavement.

His ears pricked into sharp triangles. He carried his tail jauntily, straight as a mast. He trotted away from the Forum, running purposefully to the alley. Instinctively he was off, to find a person of his own.

The alley threaded a way through walls that reared up like cliffs of broken stucco and peeling, tobacco-brown paint. Suddenly, it turned sharply to funnel out into a wide pavement where people walked, and where traffic raced along a roadway. Horns honked, cars revved, motor bikes buzzed and trucks growled. A city strada during daylight hours was not a place for cats.

Once, in kitten days, Moon-Eyes had slept on the wheel of a parked car. He had snuggled into the space between the tire and the fender. Later, when someone had opened one of the car's doors, Moon-Eyes had jumped in fright to the roadway. A skittling car with a blaring horn had almost bowled him over, as flat as a cat-rug. Since then, he had kept off the streets during the day.

So, he waited where he was. He waited and watched for a minute or so. His head poked into the street and he peered out cautiously to inspect the traffic. The rest of Moon-Eyes was safely in the alley.

Before long, the traffic came to a screeching halt. Groups of people crossed the street. Maria was with them.

The glimpse was enough to flush Moon-Eyes from the alley. Out he came. His tail limp, hanging low, lower than his haunches. He scuttled across the road, keeping close to the heels of a man. On either side cars snorted, like giant beetles, waiting to pounce.

His heart was racing when he reached the gutter on the other side. The traffic hummed on its way again. Hearing it move, Moon-Eyes didn't alter his pace. He stayed behind the man, hurrying on, until they reached a small piazza.

The man turned here and sighted the cat.
"Scram!" he said, stamping his feet. "Scram! Il gatto,
hop it!"

Moon-Eyes withdrew. His retreat was polite as
he backed into the piazza. Standing hesitantly, he
held one forepaw in front of him. He looked puzzled,
as if he'd remembered Maria again, but she was gone.
Moon-Eyes had lost her.

The wind blew, parting his fur and chilling his
thin body. Moon-Eyes shivered. The wind was
coming in gusts, willy-nilly, changing directions,
teasing him. A scrap of paper catherine-wheeled by.
Moon-Eyes shied, mewing faintly. Another flutter of
wind blew in his face, into his eyes. He shut them
defensively, then opened them at once. Trapped in
the wind-puff had been the faint aroma of food. A
tormenting, tantalizing smell of cooking!

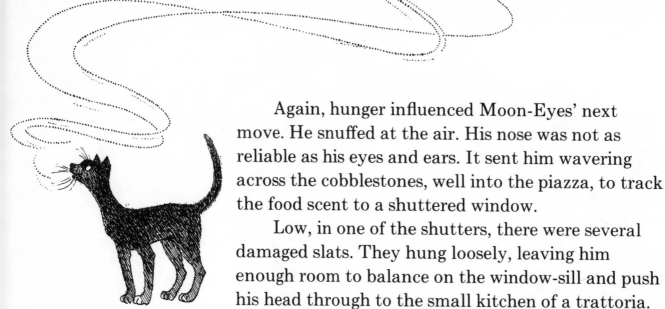

Again, hunger influenced Moon-Eyes' next move. He snuffed at the air. His nose was not as reliable as his eyes and ears. It sent him wavering across the cobblestones, well into the piazza, to track the food scent to a shuttered window.

Low, in one of the shutters, there were several damaged slats. They hung loosely, leaving him enough room to balance on the window-sill and push his head through to the small kitchen of a trattoria.

The little room smelled dizzily of fish and meat, milk and garlic and coffee. Pots simmered on a stove. And on a shaky table, almost within paw's reach, was a bowl of meaty sauce. Moon-Eyes' scratched nose wrinkled his appreciation, and his whiskers quivered with joy.

In he went, sliding through the slats as if he were a boneless cat, made from silk. One graceful leap and he was on the table, nibbling at the edge of the bowl. The sauce was hot, very hot.

Then he saw the cream — the topping on a chocolate cake.

A powerful jump took him to the shelf where the cake was stored. He lapped the richly sweet, chocolate-flavored cream. The taste? The taste stopped him licking, just long enough for his tongue to lose the regular movement of his laps, then it went to work again. Moon-Eyes might not have eaten so much of the chocolate cream if he hadn't been so hungry. Certainly, while he licked he kept glancing

sideways, down to the cooling sauce, until its
closeness became too much for him. With a soft plop,
he returned to the table and the bowl of meat sauce.

Moon-Eyes ate with neat cat-manners. His
forepaws were tucked under his chest, and he leaned
on his haunches with his tail wrapped tidily to one
side.

He had not eaten nearly enough of the sauce,
when, suddenly, as if from nowhere, a knife flew
across the kitchen. It swished over his head and
stabbed into the table, just beyond the bowl.

Moon-Eyes jerked upwards, then he fled. He had
seen the knife thrower. It was the trattoria's cook.

The man looked like a giant as he spread himself
and his rage all over the kitchen. Lurching about the
little room, he snatched up pans and ladles, anything
to use as a weapon which he hurled at the terrified
cat. "Thief! Witch cat! Pilfering little beast!" he
shouted. "I'll kill you. Keep still, you monster! I'll
get you, devil cat!"

In a fuzz of bristles Moon-Eyes scrambled to the
highest shelf in the room. He snaked behind a bottle
of oil. A copper omelette pan followed him. It hit
the bottle, hard enough to dislodge it. The bottle
teetered on the edge of the shelf. It fell. It crashed
down to the floor where shattered glass mixed with
the oil to ooze over the tiles.

Once the bottle was gone Moon-Eyes had no
protection. He faced the cook. He threw cat-abuse
at him. His hair still stood up on his neck and back,
and it turned his tail into a bottle-brush. He flicked
it sideways, towards the cook. Moon-Eyes was
making himself look as tall and as ferocious as he
could. His long legs stiffened until he seemed to be
standing on toe tips. Even his paw pads enlarged,

swelling as he drew out his claws. No longer a mild, timid cat, he squashed his nose, opened his mouth wide and snarled deeply from his chest. He was warning the cook that he was savage and wild. The cook was to lay off, unless he wanted to be torn and scratched into shreds, or worse.

The cook was ignorant of cat-talk. He threw an egg whisk as if it were a javelin, and pranced towards the spilled oil. Next thing, he was skating in it, slithering towards the table. To break his fall, the man grabbed at the table's edge. His weight dragged the table down and the sauce slid with it.

The cook yelled, and his yells were louder and more alarming to Moon-Eyes than a street filled with motor bikes.

The noise also upset a waitress who looked into the kitchen. She wheeled about, and ran through the trattoria, into the street, screaming as she went, "Police! Police! Murder! Where's the Carabiniere? Help! Murder!"

Curious passers-by followed the waitress, who rushed back indoors. She led the way to the kitchen. In turn, astonished customers left their tables to tail along. Last of all came the cashier. She locked the money drawer in her desk, and pocketed the key before she joined the crowd.

Questions! Questions! Everyone asked questions but no one knew if the cook was being murdered, or if he was doing the murdering, until they found him, sauce-spattered and staggering to his feet. "I'm all right!" he bawled out, "but don't any one of you let that cat out. I'm going to kill him. I'll screw his black neck! I'll boil him in the stew pan! I'll hang him up by his tail! I'll . . . I'll drown him in sauce!"

"Oh?" said the cashier. "You can't do all of that!"

"Of course, I can. Look at this mess! He made it. He's responsible. He deserves all I'll give him."

"Hummmp!" said the cashier.

"Big as a dog, he was. And with great glaring eyes, like saucers!" The cook shouted to his appreciative audience. "Teeth like a shark's, too. And I've seen a shark, so I know. And his claws! They were tiger's claws. *Tiger's claws*, I tell you! But I'll kill that cat. There'll be no escape for him." The cook paused to rummage in a drawer. He pulled out a carving knife. "Where is that cat?" he asked.

"There is no cat. There never was a cat like the one you saw," said the cashier.

The cook snorted in disbelief. He shrugged and threw his arms down wildly as he looked about the kitchen. And there was *no* cat! Neither was there a place where a cat could successfully hide. Everyone there could see that.

The cook stepped close to the cashier. Drawing in his breath he said evenly, "It must have escaped through the trattoria."

"No, it didn't," said the cashier. "No one has seen a monster cat with teeth like a shark's. You must have imagined it, Giuseppe. Have you been drinking?" She sniffed about him, suspiciously, then she shrilled. "You *have* been drinking, Giuseppe! So early in the day, too! You are a bad man. You will be telling me next that there are frogs swimming in the minestrone!"

"I have not been drinking. I am as sober as a baby," the cook shouted at her. "There was a cat. I saw him with my eyes, with these two things here." He pointed to his eyes.

"Then your eyes must have seen a ghost. Otherwise, how did your enormous cat get out of here?" the cashier yelled back. "I'll tell you, Giuseppe, there was no cat. Get on with your work. The matter is over, done with," she told him. "There are people waiting for service." And she turned away, smiling at the onlookers and ushering them from the kitchen.

She was the last to leave. The cook slammed the door after her. "No cat?" he questioned himself, doubtfully. "No cat? . . . I *must* have seen a cat," he quietly answered. Then he shouted, defiantly at the door, "I did see a cat! *There was a cat!*"

When Moon-Eyes had faced the maddened cook
he was playing for enough time to make his escape.
During the uproar, his chance came to slip unseen,
back through the broken shutter. He ran
arrow-straight across the piazza to the street. Then
he ran, and he ran, shadow-like; hugging so close to
the walls of the buildings that he almost brushed
against them.

He was a streamlined cat now. His body
stretched out, long and close to the ground. His tail,
level with his spine, was shafted out behind. His ears
were so flat against his head they had almost become
buried in the short fur that grew there. With this
earless look, his head rounded like a hard black ball.

Like any cat, Moon-Eyes could run in short
bursts only. Presently he slackened his speed into a
less tiring stride. He kept glancing over his shoulder,
watching for pursuit, even when he realized that the
cook hadn't followed him. As well, he carefully
avoided the dangers of open spaces, often zig-zagging
off course, to the shelter of a wall, or to a clump
of weeds, or a dustbin, or he glided into the shadows
of a doorway.

Rain fell. Veils of fine rain that blew away then drifted back again to wet the pavements and to softly wet his fur with tiny droplets of moisture. They clung to him, glinting like silvery crystal beads on pinheads of silver.

Moon-Eyes didn't seem to be aware of the rain. He was too intent upon escape. The cook's attack had renewed an inbuilt distrust of people, yet it had not blotted out the memory of Maria's gentle stroking, and the feeling of comfort it had given him. The feeling was becoming as important to him now as food and rest.

Indeed, Moon-Eyes needed a person of his own.

Gradually he calmed down and his flight ended under a bush, close to a church. People were here. He stared out at them, from his refuge. His eyes rounded, and he watched the people waiting in the cloister.

The cloister bordered the stone wall of the church, which had stood for hundreds of years, its foundations in a corner of the Forum. Long ago, the oldest section of the church had been a temple to an ancient god. Then generations of Romans had built over it and around it, until it had risen into a great building, famous for its architecture, its age, its treasured mosaics and its presepio.

When compared with the church's age the presepio was almost modern. Even so, it was at least two hundred years since it had been created for a

family, perhaps with many children. That was in
Naples. Eventually, the presepio had been brought
across Italy to Rome.

It was a whimsical portrayal of the first
Christmas. The Three Wise Men, bearing their gifts,
were gathered before the Holy Family. All of the
figures were richly robed, and all were splendid with
jewels. The stable was grand, too. It was not a
humble shed for animals, but a lofty arch flanked
by slender columns, above which soared a flight of
angels, spiraling into a blue sky. This was not
Bethlehem. The scene could have been set in the
Forum, or some other ruin, except that the stable was
surrounded on all sides by an Italian village.

Tall farmhouses dotted the hills where the grass
was green and pine trees grew. There was a castle
and there were squat, crenellated towers. There were
broken arches and pillars and crumbling brick walls,
which were a reminder of the Forum's faded
grandeur.

And up and down the cobbled streets, in and out
of doorways and windows, peasants were busy with
their daily tasks. Farmers trimmed vines, shepherds
moved sheep, and a bare-footed man climbed a
walnut tree to harvest the crop. Women nursed
babies, or washed, or baked, carried water, or sewed,
while children played and the village gossips met.

Everyone was up and about, doing something.

There was so much to see and enjoy. The presepio was large enough to take up one whole wall of the church. And it was famous enough for people to defy the Christmas cold, to line up with their children waiting for their turn to see it.

The line halted frequently, before dribbling forward again. And the large number of people made Moon-Eyes uncertain. He couldn't settle. His tail twitched, then a shoulder. He kneaded the ground with his claws. It was cold and damp.

Moon-Eyes was bone-weary and he needed a better place to sleep. No one cared; no one was interested when he ran behind the line and turned a corner of the church. Furtive little cats were commonplace in this part of the city. Besides, the waiting people were being entertained by the two musicians, standing in a doorway, with their tootling and wailing instruments. They were shepherds from the hills. The men came each year, bringing their Christmas music with them, to Rome.

Both were warmly dressed in old-time bulky pants and sheepskin jerkins, but the fingers that coaxed the sweet notes from the old wooden flute were chafed from cold. And the piper's cheeks, energetically puffing the bass drone from his bagpipes, were fretted and reddened by the winds. Yet their music was gay, lively, toe-tapping. The people loved it. The old peasant carols set bodies swaying, and encouraged a few to hum their melodies. Coins dropped into the bowl at the shepherd's feet, or a thousand lira note fluttered down as the appreciative families filed into the church.

Moon-Eyes could still hear the shepherds' carols when he discovered the partly opened door, a little door dwarfed by the church walls.

He stood on its threshold and shook each sodden paw, then he looked into the pocket-sized room. It was empty, except for some mops and buckets and a couple of brooms. Moon-Eyes didn't go in immediately. He listened for a moment longer, then he padded inside, across bare boards.

The place smelled dank, and there was a nose-twitching, lip-licking scent of mice. But it was a disappointingly stale smell. A fading, musky whiff of a long-departed mouse family.

He settled on a mop. It was soft and cozily dry. His tail folded over his scratched nose, over the wound which had hardened into threads of dried blood, as small as machine stitches. A little cat ball of fur, Moon-Eyes dozed fitfully.

Somewhere, far off, a hum of voices mingled with the shepherds' lilting. As the sounds came no closer the cat was lulled into a feeling of security. He drifted into a deeper sleep which lasted for an hour, or longer.

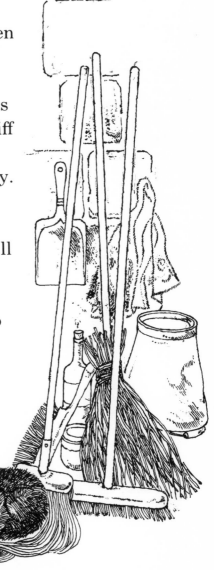

Rude pokings from a birch broom wakened
Moon-Eyes. A cleaning woman scolded as she
prodded him, and she kept prodding, following
Moon-Eyes with the broom when he indignantly
leaped across the room. *Poke-push!* The woman
cornered him between a bucket and a wall. Her
broom prickled through his fur to tender skin.
Prod-prod-prod! Swooooosh! He was swept from the
corner to the door, as if he were a heap of dust, or
dried leaves. She was determined to slither him out
into the cold, unwelcoming wet of the gray afternoon.

Moon-Eyes struggled. He gained his feet, rode the birch twigs for an instant and was shaken off. He turned broadside, prancing backwards, away from the broom. Then, he whipped around. Moon-Eyes became a flying cat. Up, over the broom! He sprang behind the woman and skimmed through a narrow doorway. It was a cupboard. He almost collided with its back wall. Without a pause, he pivoted, and, as graceful as a dancer, he swirled back into the room. Out of it! Through another door! Then he was in a long corridor.

The trouncing broom and the woman chased him. Moon-Eyes ran, panic-stricken. He reached the end of the corridor and saw no way out of it. He turned, doubled-back, ducking under the broom to run on, into another passageway. It took him to yet another hallway, and finally into a large room.

He had joined the mass of people viewing the presepio. They barred his escape; to the frantic cat their legs and umbrellas were as thick as a forest of spindly trees.

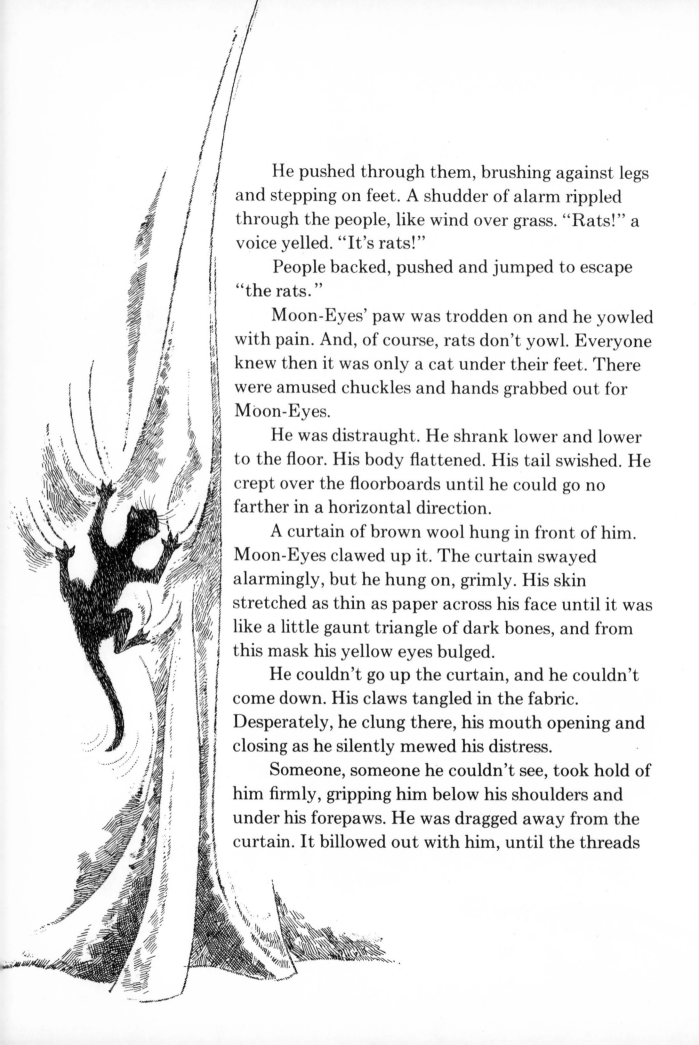

He pushed through them, brushing against legs and stepping on feet. A shudder of alarm rippled through the people, like wind over grass. "Rats!" a voice yelled. "It's rats!"

People backed, pushed and jumped to escape "the rats."

Moon-Eyes' paw was trodden on and he yowled with pain. And, of course, rats don't yowl. Everyone knew then it was only a cat under their feet. There were amused chuckles and hands grabbed out for Moon-Eyes.

He was distraught. He shrank lower and lower to the floor. His body flattened. His tail swished. He crept over the floorboards until he could go no farther in a horizontal direction.

A curtain of brown wool hung in front of him. Moon-Eyes clawed up it. The curtain swayed alarmingly, but he hung on, grimly. His skin stretched as thin as paper across his face until it was like a little gaunt triangle of dark bones, and from this mask his yellow eyes bulged.

He couldn't go up the curtain, and he couldn't come down. His claws tangled in the fabric. Desperately, he clung there, his mouth opening and closing as he silently mewed his distress.

Someone, someone he couldn't see, took hold of him firmly, gripping him below his shoulders and under his forepaws. He was dragged away from the curtain. It billowed out with him, until the threads

snapped. The freed curtain swung back as
Moon-Eyes, upside down, was passed over the heads
of the crowd. His legs and claws flayed at the air
and he growled.

He was tossed through the doorway, into the
cloister.

Moon-Eyes flipped in mid-air to land on his feet.
He skidded on an icy-cold step, then he bolted. As
he rushed along the path he was followed by the
laughter of the shepherds.

The cat was so bewildered, so frightened that his
instincts began to betray him. He ran aimlessly,
without direction, away from the Forum and the
streets that he knew. He wandered through the
remainder of the afternoon with a few brief rests
before he ran on again, rarely looking anywhere but
straight ahead.

Although he was very hungry, Moon-Eyes made no attempt to hunt a careless bird, and he passed dustbins without searching them for scraps.

The dreary afternoon was deepening into dusk.

A browned leaf, a stubborn remnant of the autumn, was blown from a plane tree. It sailed downwards, to brush across Moon-Eyes' back. The touch, light as thistledown, was a caress, a reminder of a stroking hand. He remembered the comfort of Maria's kindness, hazily, as if it were a dream. His meeting with her seemed to be long ago.

Moon-Eyes' day had been too long. He had been on the move for most of it, during the time when the Forum cats slept. The pads of his feet were sore. His pace slowed and he was quickly chilled by wind and cold.

The unhappy little cat doubled back, retracing his tracks, making for his home territory. He travelled on into the dusk, too weary to be sure of his way to the Forum.

Then, as if he could go no farther, Moon-Eyes crept through a deserted archway, into a building. It was another church. Probably the silent, cave-like gloom behind the entrance attracted him. The soft darkness promised a hiding place that would be warmer than the streets.

Behind Moon-Eyes, the city lights flickered,

then deepened into wide halos of brightness. Up and down the fashionable stradas, elegant street decorations competed with the glittering displays in the shops and stores.

The plate-glass entrance to an embassy was filled with a tall Christmas tree. It glowed with candles, shimmered with baubles and was cheerfully bright with red apples and snowy popcorn-chains.

Ignoring the bleakness of the coming night, the bagpiper and the shepherd with the flute moved away to the Spanish Steps where another presepio was flood-lit and attracting fresh crowds of visitors. The wind was stronger and the rain more persistent, but it would be a busy night for the shepherds. Their carols would bring more coins clinking into the wooden bowl. People were generous. Christmas was a time to give.

Farther away, in the Forum, the cats were waking. They stretched and prepared for the nightly mouse hunts. Later on, when the Cat Woman came with her pasta, she might bring a little fish, or a scrap of meat for the luckiest cat.

And all over Rome, priests were making ready for the evening services in their churches.

A brown-robed Franciscan monk was moving silently through his church, lighting the tall candles. Pencil-thin flares of light shot up from the wicks, then dwindled downward into plump, tear-shaped flames that glowed on the shabby frescoes

decorating the church walls. The golden light
deepened the colors of the faded paint and
smoothed the torn edges of chipped plaster.

Under a fresco, on one wall, a niche framed a
presepio. It was a small scene, bare of details, except
for those that belonged to the shepherds in the
Christmas story. Mary and Joseph, and Baby Jesus
had been carved from pearwood. The simple figures
had a dignified grace and were satin-smooth from the
craftsman's art, and from years of loving
handling. Shepherds, thigh-deep in straw, knelt
before the rough manger that cradled the Child.
One shepherd held a lamb. Another carried his
bagpipes.

The natural browns of the wood and the cream
of the straw added to the serene beauty of the
presepio, even though it was harshly lit by a single
electric bulb that dangled to one side of the figures.

A few people were in the church. They paused
by the presepio, and no matter how brief was their
stay, they turned away, smiling.

Soon, a grandmother hurried into the church.
She was cocooned inside a thick black coat, and her
face was almost hidden by scarves. She wasn't much
taller than the two little boys who came with her.
They pushed through the heavy draft curtains,
which kept out some of the cold, bobbed into hasty
genuflections, crossed themselves as quickly as they
dared under their Nonna's watchful eyes, then
half-walked, half-skipped to the presepio.

Their Nonna knelt, praying over her rosary. Her beads clicked and her lips murmured words she had learned as a child, but she was distracted. The children were making too much noise. She looked towards them several times and made *tsking* sounds. The noise went on, excitedly. Nonna waggled a finger, then came to the presepio. "Hush! Hush now!" she told the boys.

"Nonna! Come and see," they told her. *"Looooook!"*

"Yes, yes! I am looking. I see the Babe and I see . . .!" She broke off, speechless for the moment, surprised by what she saw. Then, clucking with disapproval, Nonna untangled from the children to swoop down on the priest.

Nonna had come to the church all her life. Now, in her seventies, she visited the church daily. It was her self-imposed task to help with the running of things. Everything had to be perfect, especially now at Christmas.

In a torrent of whispers she spoke urgently to the priest. He listened gravely, leaning towards her. Then, with Nonna still hissing her complaint, he brought her back to the presepio. "This is not right," Nonna said. "You can see that? Now, what will the good Lord up above us think?" she asked. "This is an insult to His Holy Family!"

"But Nonna, it is only a new animal in the stable, that's all," one of the boys said.

"I wonder where he came from?" asked the other.

"Wherever it was, he can go back there again," declared Nonna. *"Sppppt!"* She leaned into the presepio, to hunt off the intruder. *"Sppppt!"*

The priest restrained her gently. "Let him be," he said. "He came to find warmth and rest, so Nonna, we shall let him sleep to his fill. Later, when he wakes, we'll find him some soup to warm his insides."

"Then, the cat can stay here? Really?" the boys wanted to know.

"It is *not* right!" insisted Nonna. "You cannot allow that. He may . . . he may dirty the presepio. It is not right."

"Nonna, who can say there was not a cat in the Bethlehem stable, long ago?" the priest asked her.

"Aaaaaaah!" Nonna's face crinkled into a crazing of fine lines. She was smiling, liking the priest's question. "Who can say?" she nodded up at him. "I learn something new with each day," she chuckled. "Yes, yes, I see. I see. Animals shared their shelter then, and now the Christ Child shares his presepio with a cat." Nonna was pleased with her spoken thought. Her satisfied chuckle deepened and she stepped closer to the presepio, looking down at the little black intruder.

He was curled on the straw, under the heat from the unshaded light. "I don't suppose he was warm until he came here," she decided. "And look at his nose! Is that a scratch?"

The cat flicked an ear. He opened an eye drowsily.

The priest leaned across and fondled one of his ears. "Something has scratched him," he told Nonna as he slipped his hand down the cat's back in a firm stroke.

The cat sat upright, propped on his forepaws. His neck curved upwards to the fondling hand. His eyes, as round and as yellow as a pale full moon, opened widely, trustingly, then they shut again, as, with a short nudging movement, he nuzzled against the hand. Moon-Eyes looked ecstatic.

The children bunched closer to the blissful cat,
almost climbing into the presepio with him. He made
no attempt to scurry away from their eager hands,
wanting to pet him.

The cat was sensing a feeling of warmth and
kindness from these people. There was nothing here
to make him feel afraid, or even cautious.

Moon-Eyes' search was over. He had not found
a person of his own, but four people had found him.
And they assumed that he would stay in the church
as long as he wanted to stay.

He settled in, at that moment.

Soon he was a fat cat. His sleek fur looked
blacker than Nonna's winter coat. He was her
presepio cat, and she brought him tidbits of fish, or
meat when she could spare them. And there was
always good food from the priests' kitchen.
Moon-Eyes was excellently fed. He peacefully ate
each meal, without the risk of it being stolen from
under his nose. And there were mice. It was his
business to keep as many of them as he could from
the church. He hunted, and in his way helped Nonna
and the priests.

When he was off duty, Moon-Eyes had a
favorite spot, in the sun, on the church steps, or he
dozed by the kitchen stove.

He learned to answer to many names. There was
il gattino and *little brother* from the priests. Nonna
called him *Putti*. And the children called him
Moon-Eyes. It was the name that suited him best.

There was nothing more the little black cat
could need.

GLOSSARY

bambina	A little girl. A little boy is a *bambino*
Carabiniere	Policeman
Forum	A public place where markets and Courts of Justice are held. The Roman Forum has been in ruins for many centuries
il gatto	The cat
il gattino	The kitten
minestrone	Thick Italian soup usually made of vegetables, pork or bacon, and cooked for a long time
Nonna	Grandmother